Wing Nut

— MJ Auch —

Wing Nut

Henry Holt and Company
New York

Special thanks to Louise Chambers, education
coordinator for the Purple Martin Conservation
Association and associate editor of the *Purple Martin Update*
magazine, and Casey Evans-Cable, associate editor of the
Purple Martin Update magazine, for making sure that Charlie
Fernwald got his purple martin facts straight.
Grady Flood's cherished book is *The Great Gilly Hopkins*
by Katherine Paterson.

Henry Holt and Company, LLC
Publishers since 1866
115 West 18th Street
New York, New York 10011
www.henryholt.com

Henry Holt is a registered trademark of Henry Holt and Company, LLC
Copyright © 2005 by Mary Jane Auch
All rights reserved.
Distributed in Canada by H. B. Fenn and Company Ltd.

Library of Congress Cataloging-in-Publication Data
Auch, Mary Jane.
Wing nut / MJ Auch.—1st ed.
p.   cm.
Summary: When twelve-year-old Grady and his mother relocate yet again, they find
work taking care of an elderly man, who teaches Grady about cars, birds, and what it
means to have a home.
ISBN-13: 978-0-8050-7531-1
ISBN-10: 0-8050-7531-3
[1. Moving, Household—Fiction.   2. Mothers and sons—Fiction.
3. Home—Fiction.   4. Old age—Fiction.]   I. Title.
PZ7.A898Wg 2005
[Fic]—dc22   2004054046

First edition—2005
Printed in the United States of America on acid-free paper.∞

1   3   5   7   9   10   8   6   4   2

To Pat Lynch, my purple martin mentor, who has shown endless patience in helping me with this book and with my efforts to start a purple martin colony. Her untiring dedication to her own thriving martin colony qualifies her as a certifiable "wing nut."

Wing
Nut

CHAPTER
1

Grady Flood couldn't stand the heat of the flames on his face another second. He turned and slipped away from the group that circled the fire. Tonight was the Sunward Path Commune's first bonfire meeting of the year, which Grady knew meant at least a couple hours of boring discussion followed by endless singing. Now that it was April, the weekly meetings could be held outside, which was better than being crowded into the living room of the dilapidated farmhouse. Ever since he turned twelve a few months ago, Grady was considered an adult. He was required to attend meetings, but nobody could force him to listen.

The air was damp with dew as he walked through the darkness up the short driveway to the barn, just far enough away to let his mind wander without getting disapproving looks from the others. Grady settled on a bale of hay and leaned his tired back against the barn wall. He'd spent most of the day transplanting scrawny broccoli plants into the garden. Every muscle in his body ached, which didn't seem fair because he hated broccoli. But then, nothing at Sunward Path was fair.

"Wham! You're dead!" Grady was struck from the side, sending him sprawling on the ground. It was Tran, one of the younger commune boys. Tran was short for Tranquility, which Grady considered the worst case of misnaming a kid he had ever seen.

"I caught the monster," Tran crowed, pummeling Grady on the back. "Die, monster, die!"

Grady twisted around and captured the four-year-old in a hammerlock. "Hey, quiet down, Tran. You want to get us both in trouble?" Grady knew that was an empty threat. The little kids at Sunward Path couldn't get in trouble for anything short of murder, and even then, they'd probably get the benefit of the doubt.

Sunward Path was only one more in a series of dead-end places Grady and Lila had stayed since his father had died seven years ago. Grady had been five at the time. He did the math again in his head to make sure it was right. More than half of his life had been on the move, and the only thing that stayed constant was Lila.

He looked at his mother now, standing among the others. The orange firelight made her long wavy red hair look like it was flame itself. Grady was sure she could be a movie star if they could only make their way out to Hollywood. But Lila had never even tried to get them to California. Instead they had moved around through the Midwest, where she had slaved away at one low-paying job after another. Lila put up with a lot—more than Grady thought she should tolerate—but sooner or later something would get her upset enough to leave, and they'd pack up and take off without having a clue where they were headed.

Grady had a rating system for the places they stayed—ten for the best, one for the worst. Sunward Path was barely a three. They never had stayed at a one or two. A one would mean no food and no bed. Two would be either food or shelter, not both. But since Lila always looked for a job that would give them meals and a place to live, they had never sunk below the level of a three.

Tran wiggled loose from Grady's grip and ran off, but Grady knew he'd be back. There were six kids on the commune, ranging in age from two to seven, and they were pretty much allowed to roam at will. An outsider would have a hard time matching up the six kids with the fifteen adults. Since nobody else seemed to care, Grady had taken it upon himself to make sure none of the little guys got hurt. It wasn't an easy job, especially when he had chores to do. But the kids seemed to sense that Grady cared about them, and he usually had two or three of them following him around as if he were the Pied Piper.

Grady always felt it was his job to protect creatures smaller and more helpless than himself. Didn't matter if they were people or animals. His father had been like that. Anytime somebody found a starving stray dog or an injured wild animal they'd bring it to Arlan Flood. His dad once said he should put up a sign that read "When your car or animal stops running, bring it here. Whatever's broke, we'll fix it."

Grady liked the fact that he had inherited that talent from his father. Arlan Flood had been a big bear of a man, not exactly the kind you'd picture talking in a high little voice while he pulled a splinter from a dog's paw with tweezers, especially since his normal voice sounded more like the blast from an eighteen-wheeler's horn. It always seemed strange to Grady that Lila, who already had a soft, gentle voice, wasn't much good at animal saving. She had such a tender heart, all she ever could do was watch over his dad's shoulder and cry. Not that she was a softie all the time. When she got mad about something, she was like a terrier on a rat.

Grady noticed that the voices around the fire were raised in some sort of an argument, and Lila seemed to be right in the middle of it. He ran back to the group to find out what was going on.

"I can't do this no more," Lila was saying. In the firelight, her cheeks were shiny with tears. "When we first come here, everybody did their share, but now all the cooking and cleaning up falls to me. It's not fair."

Rayden, the commune leader, moved around the circle to put his arm across Lila's shoulders. "Lila, Lila, my dear child. You must understand that things have changed in the months you have been here. We used to be a group of workers, with only one or two philosophers, but now"—his arm gesture swept the circle—"philosophy has become our main focus."

Grady let out a little snort of disgust. Rayden had himself all dressed up to look like Jesus, if you could ignore his nose ring, the snake tattoo winding around his ankle, and the cell phone antenna sticking out of his burlap caftan pocket.

Rayden gave Grady a sharp look, then turned back to Lila. "We count on our group of workers to keep the community functioning to allow the others time for a higher purpose. Of course cooking and washing the dishes is every bit as important as finding the meaning of life, but we each must know our place and accept it." His little speech sounded like he was talking to someone Tran's age. Rayden smiled at the end to show everybody what a good guy he was. What a crock, Grady thought.

Grady heard the sharp intake of air that meant Lila was gearing up to let loose with her temper. Sure enough, Lila pushed Rayden's arm from her shoulders. "You know what, Rayden? You don't have no group of workers. You got me and Grady, and maybe one or two others, who work when the spirit moves them, which isn't very often. Only now you don't even have that, because Grady and me are getting out of here."

Grady squeezed in beside his mother, noticing that his shoulder was only a few inches lower than hers. In spite of the hard work, or maybe because of it, he'd grown a lot in the eight months they'd been here. He wedged himself firmly between Lila and the sweet-talking Rayden. Grady never had trusted that man. Something about Rayden's creepy smile and oily voice made the hairs stand up on the back of his neck. Grady's "crook, cheater, and no-good phony" radar had grown much sharper than his mother's, and he had pegged Rayden for all three right from the beginning.

The other commune members were whispering among themselves now. Tran and his little brother raced around inside the circle, playing tag. Not one of the adults stepped forward to keep the youngsters' bare feet from stepping on the hot coals that had rolled away from the edges of the fire. Grady grabbed the boys as they ran by, then deposited them in front of their mother. "You gotta take care of your kids," he said. "They could get hurt."

The young mother smiled dreamily. "Mother Earth takes care of her own."

"Well, Mother Earth is a lousy babysitter," Grady said, "because I been saving their hides at least a dozen times a day. You gotta watch 'em yerself from now on because I'm not gonna be here. They get in a lot of trouble when they're on their own."

Lila had left the circle and was headed toward the house. Grady ran to catch up, thinking how lucky he was to have a mother who had always looked after him. "You mean it, Mom, right? We're really taking off?"

"Oh, you bet I mean it." Lila's face was red, either from the heat of the fire or from anger. "They can do their high-and-mighty philosophizing all they want, but when their bellies are empty and the garbage and dirty dishes are piled up to the ceiling, maybe they'll wake up." Her voice bumped with each step as she slammed her heels into the ground. "Bunch of no-account snobs. Think they're smart just because their rich daddies sent them to college. I could teach every last one of them a thing or two about common sense."

Grady heard someone coming fast behind them in the dark. It was Russ, the new guy who'd been sniffing around Lila since the day he'd arrived about a month ago. He had come to Sunward Path to do research for a college paper comparing today's communes with the ones from the sixties or some darn fool thing like that. He was somebody else Grady didn't trust, but Lila was usually nice to him. Heck, she was nice to everybody until she saw through them. Russ caught her arm. "Lila, you aren't really thinking of leaving, are you?"

"Just watch me." Lila didn't break her stride.

"But where will you go?"

"Who knows? Anything's better than here."

Lila pushed the front door to the house so hard it smacked against the wall. Grady had to sidestep fast to keep from getting hit as the door bounced back. His mother was already up the stairs and into their room by the time he got into the house. As he reached their doorway, she tossed him his backpack. "Gather up all your stuff. We're leaving tonight. I wanna be out of here before those fools get back from the bonfire."

That wouldn't be hard. They hardly had any belongings to pack. Grady started scavenging under his bunk for stray socks. He only had five altogether, none of them mates. Heck, no two were even the same size. As Grady resurfaced from under the bed, he could hear the faint sound of singing coming up from the bonfire. Once the Sunward Path gang got started with the music, it could go on for hours. He and Lila would be long gone before anybody missed them.

Grady felt around the back edge of his mattress until he found the slit where he hid his two treasures—a worn-out paperback book and a little red Corvette. The two things he loved most in the world, next to his mother, were reading and cars. Not that he'd had much chance for reading here. The commune had an orange crate bookshelf with a few dusty old volumes on it, but as much as Grady tried, he couldn't make sense out of any of those books. So he read and reread his own book, discovering new things in the story each time.

"Don't be sitting there daydreaming," Lila said. "Let's go."

Grady stuffed the book and car into his backpack and took the stairs two at a time, trying to catch up with his mother. When he burst out into the damp night air, she was already in the car. Grady threw his pack into the backseat and slid in next to her.

"I sure hope they didn't run me out of gas," Lila said. Ever since Lila and Grady had arrived with their own car, the other commune members had been borrowing it to drive into town. First it was just once in a while. Then it was almost every day. Grady and Lila had both stopped noticing when it was taken, because nobody had bothered to ask permission for several months now.

Lila turned the key, but nothing happened. She banged her open palm against the steering wheel.

Grady started to get out. "No problem, Mom. I'll go siphon some gas out of the tractor."

Lila closed her eyes and leaned her head back on the seat. "It's not gas, Grady. The engine won't even turn over." She hit the steering wheel again. "How could I be so stupid? It's my car. I shoulda took better care of it. Your daddy always said you have to treat a car like a member of the family."

Russ knocked on the driver's-side window. "Your car has been on the fritz for a couple weeks now, Lila. Want me to take a look at it for you?"

"You know anything about engines, Russ?"

Russ shrugged. "I took a six-week mechanics course in junior high. It's not rocket science, you know."

"Okay, give it a try. We sure can't walk out of here." She slid over to make room for him.

Russ moved in close to her. "Maybe I could go along with you. Grady could use a father figure. Somebody to guide him on the path to becoming a man." He leaned forward over the steering wheel to grin at Grady.

Grady seethed with anger at that remark, as well as the one about auto mechanics not being rocket science. Grady's father had been the best mechanic in Mason County. Everybody had said so. And he had promised to teach Grady everything he knew, but then he died before he had a chance to do it. Grady would give anything to have his dad's mechanical skills, and now this jerk was making that sound like nothing. He got out of the car and closed the passenger door a lot harder than he needed to.

Lila gently pushed Russ away. "We'll talk about that later, Russ. Right now we got to get this car back on the road." She slid over to the passenger window. "We're not going anywhere tonight, Grady. Go on up to the room and get some sleep. Tomorrow's gonna be a big day."

"Why don't you come with me, Mom? You need sleep, too." Russ was trying to raise the hood. Grady glared at him. No way that jerk was going to be his dad.

"I'll stay and help Russ with the car." Lila got out and pulled their packs from the backseat. "Here, take my stuff up with yours." She pressed her forehead against Grady's and gave his arm a little squeeze as she handed him the bag.

"Mo-om," Grady whispered. "You gotta watch out for this guy. He's pure trouble."

"Russ'll give up on the car if I don't keep him working. I can take care of myself, Grady. Just you go in and leave me be."

Grady went up to the room, but he didn't even try to sleep. As much as he wanted to get away from Sunward Path, at least he knew how to deal with the people here. Whenever they moved on to a new place, Grady felt as if he and Lila were two cartoon characters accidentally running off the edge of a cliff. Lila was the lighthearted one who could do a double take, turn, and run through the air to land back on the cliff. Grady was the one who always felt the gravity of their situation. He dropped like a stone every time.

Grady ran his hand around the inside of the backpack to find his book. It was so worn from reading, the edges of the pages were three times as thick as the spine. The book was about a girl named Gilly Hopkins who had been shipped around to a lot of foster homes, always hoping she'd end up with her mother. Grady had never been much for reading until he got that book. It was comforting to find another kid who was worse off than him, even if she was only a made-up character. Gilly wanted to be with her mother real bad. No matter how many times Grady got moved and no matter where he got shuffled to, he always had his mom right there with him. So that made him better off than Gilly.

The book had belonged to a library two doors down from where they lived when Lila worked as a waitress. The librarian had shown him lots of other books that were okay, but once he read *The Great Gilly Hopkins,* he kept taking it out over and over. One day, when he was checking it out again, the librarian said, "This book can't hold up to being taken out many more times, Grady." He went there so often, she knew his name. He knew her name, too— Mrs. Parravano. He liked the way it sounded like music when he said it. He had a sick feeling in his stomach that day. He didn't know what he would do if Mrs. Parravano wouldn't let him take out the book anymore. He *needed* that book, especially when he was plunging off that cliff. It kept him from hitting the bottom.

Mrs. Parravano had smiled at him. "Paperback books don't hold up as well as the hardcovers." She had taken it out of his hands. "You love this book so much, you should keep it. And I can show you lots of other books that you'll enjoy reading." Grady had held his breath, afraid he hadn't heard her right, but sure enough, she wrote DISCARD on the inside of the front cover and handed it to him.

He had clutched the book to his chest, too happy to find any words but "thank you," which didn't come anywhere close to the gratitude he was feeling. Nobody but Lila and his dad had ever given him a present. He didn't understand why Mrs. Parravano thought paper-back books weren't as good as the ones with hard cov-ers. A hardcover book seemed all stiff and serious, but an old familiar paperback was friendlier, fluffing up its pages like it was trying to open itself up to make you read it. Grady knew Gilly Hopkins so well, he could start on almost any page and jump right into the story without missing a beat, so he often set the book down on its spine and let the book choose the starting point for him.

Grady and Lila had moved away from that town a few days after Mrs. Parravano gave him his book. He never had a chance to say good-bye to the librarian. That was a shame, because he had thought of a better way to thank her. He wanted to say, "This book makes me feel safe," which was exactly right. But he probably would have been embarrassed to say that to her. And she might not have understood what he meant anyway, seeing as how she lived a pretty wonderful life, working in the library and all.

Grady stretched out on his lumpy cot and scrunched up the backpack to make a pillow. The book had opened to the part where Gilly was meeting a new kid in the foster home. The bare bulb hanging from the ceiling didn't throw enough light to read by, but Grady didn't need to see the words anymore to picture what was happening. He felt his breathing slow as he entered Gilly's world and played out the scene in his head.

He was distracted by a fly buzzing around the lightbulb. Then it zinged past his ear and hit the window screen, bouncing against it a few times with a metallic ping. Grady gently trapped the fly under his cupped hands, then slowly moved it to a hole in the screen, where it made its escape. "I'm getting away from here, too," he whispered, "first thing tomorrow morning."

Grady pivoted on his cot so he could lean on the windowsill, trying to hear what Lila and Russ were saying down below. The flames from the bonfire cast weird dancing shadows on the wall of the barn beyond. All Grady could make out was the low murmur of Lila's voice and the occasional clang of a wrench over a background of "Kumbaya." On about the thirty-seventh verse of "Kumbaya," he drifted off to sleep.

CHAPTER 2

When Grady woke up the next morning, the sky was barely tinged with pink. He was still in his clothes, stretched out full length on his cot with the windowsill digging into his cheek. He felt a sharp pain on the side of his neck as he slung the backpacks over his shoulder. When he got outside, Russ was working under the hood and Lila was behind the wheel.

Grady slid into the passenger seat and scrunched down so Russ wouldn't notice him. "He been working on this all night?"

Lila yawned and stretched. "No. Russ wanted to go back for the singing, so I slept in the car for a while. Then he wanted a nap, so he ain't been working on it more'n an hour or two. I think he's getting close, though. He's got it to turn over now, but it keeps stalling out." She ran her fingers over the indentation in Grady's cheek. "What did you do to yourself?"

Grady pulled away. "I slept wrong, is all. You don't look so good neither. You shoulda got more sleep."

She pinched the bridge of her nose—a sign that she had a headache. "I got some. Enough."

"That ought to hold her, Lila," Russ called. He came around to Grady's window. "If it starts cutting out on you again, make sure the hose is taped on tight to the carburetor. Grady, come here so I can show you this."

"I don't know nothing about engines," Grady mumbled, hoping Russ would let him alone. No such luck. Russ pulled the car door open so fast Grady almost fell out on the dirt driveway. "You don't need to know anything about engines. All you need to know is where to put the tape."

Grady looked back at his mother and asked a quick sign language question. "Is Russ coming with us?" It wasn't official sign language—just a way Grady and Lila had learned to communicate over the years when they were in a tight spot. It was done mostly with head tilts, shoulder shrugs, and eyebrows.

Lila's return gesture said, "No, he's not coming

with us. Let him show you about the car." A weight lifted from Grady's shoulders. He was almost cheerful, letting Russ explain about the hose.

"You got that, Grady?"

"Yeah, I got it. Russ, you sure are some kind of duct tape genius."

Russ looked pleased at Grady's false compliment. He smiled and ruffled Grady's hair in a fatherly gesture. Grady slipped away fast and got back in the car.

Russ slammed the hood closed and leaned down to Lila's window. "You sure you won't change your mind about me coming along? It isn't easy for a woman being alone on the road."

"She's not alone," Grady said, clenching his fist on the car seat.

Lila slipped her hand over Grady's. "We'll be fine, Russ. Thanks for your help."

Grady understood. No sense in having a fight with Russ now. It would only slow them down getting out of here.

Russ waggled his finger at Lila's dangly earring, making it send little sparkles of early morning sunlight over the dusty dashboard. "Well, if you change your mind about you and me getting together, you know where to find me." As he zeroed in to kiss Lila, Grady wished he had the button to close the window on Russ's neck. Darn thing didn't work anyway. Everything fancy on this car had worn out long ago.

Grady kept his eyes straight ahead as they backed out of the driveway.

Lila looked over at him. "The least you could do is wave good-bye, Grady. If Russ hadn't fixed the car for us, we wouldn't be going nowhere today."

"Russ don't know beans about cars. He's not Dad, you know. And I don't need a new dad, so don't be having a fool like Russ hang around with us on my account."

Grady said that to be mean—to see the way the corners of Lila's lips twitched down every time she thought of his dad, even after so much time had passed since the accident. He was sorry the second the words left his mouth. He didn't want to hurt his mother, but sometimes when he couldn't keep the edges of his world together, he took out his own panic on her.

If only Lila wasn't so darn pretty. Her red hair was real, not from a bottle, and her eyes were green— at least they looked that way when she was wearing her green sweater. She pulled guys in like flies on honey. She didn't even notice she was doing it, which made Grady nuts because he saw every look she got from men, and he knew what those looks meant. Grady wondered how long it took for a mom to get old and kind of ugly. It couldn't happen fast enough to suit him.

Lila fumbled in the compartment under the radio and fished out an old pair of sunglasses with only one ear wire. "I don't know why you'd think I'd let Russ take your father's place. Arlan Flood was my onliest ever true love. You get one of them in your whole lifetime, and some people never even find theirs. There ain't going to be nobody else, Grady. Only you and me."

Grady wished he could believe that, because they'd be fine, just the two of them. But there was always some guy wanting to butt in. And they all thought they had a perfect right to boss Grady around. Wherever they were going now, another Russ would be waiting to open the car door for Lila before she had turned off the engine.

Lila pulled out onto the main highway and picked up speed. "Here we go again, Grady. Off to a new life.

Look at that sign—'Welcome to Ohio'—like they knew we was coming."

Grady looked at the mirror in his visor and read the Welcome to Kentucky sign backward. He didn't care if he ever saw Kentucky again. He didn't care if he ever saw most of the places they'd been again. "Where are we headed this time?" He knew it must be east, because they were driving right into the sun. That seemed like a bad omen—another sunward path.

"How about New York?" Lila asked.

That got Grady's attention. "New York City? Doesn't it cost a lot to live there?"

"No, silly. Not the city. The state. New York for a New Life. Has a nice ring, don't it?"

"I guess. Long as you can find work."

This was the part that worried Grady every time. Lila always took off with no idea of how she could earn a living. In the past five years they had lived on two communes; three different houses where they had a room and Lila was a cook, a housekeeper, or both; and a room upstairs over a restaurant where Lila worked as a waitress for the room, tips, and all the food they could eat.

"We can't end up at a commune," Grady said. "I'd

starve before I'd go to another place like Sunward Path."

"They were mostly nice people, Grady, at least at first. And they taught us how to live off the land."

"Yeah, land that grew nothin' but broccoli and turnips!"

Lila smiled, knocking the one-eared glasses on an angle. "I think we were there the wrong time of year. If we'd stayed on until summer, there would have been tomatoes and squash and stuff."

Grady rolled his eyes. "Well, we better turn ourselves right around and go back there, because you didn't tell me I was missing out on squash."

Lila laughed and gave him a poke on the arm. "You wait. In a few days, we'll have a roof over our heads and all our meals for free. Don't I always find us somethin' good?" She started bobbing her head to the rhythm of a song on the radio, setting the earring sparkles in motion again and knocking the sunglasses almost clean off her face.

"You don't get nothin' for free, Mom. There's always a catch."

"Grady Flood, what makes you think that way? You can't believe something good will happen to us?"

She gave up on the broken sunglasses and tossed them into the backseat.

"I know you don't get something for nothing, is all. Things might look like they're free, but then after you get 'em, you have to pay somehow. Like the candy they gave me in that Bible school in Indiana, but then I had to listen to all that preaching stuff."

"A little preaching never hurt nobody. Probably better for you than the candy." She lifted her chin and stared straight at the road ahead. Grady could tell he had hurt her feelings again. Lila was an optimist, always looking for the best in everybody, which was why she ended up being friends with losers like Russ. She was always telling Grady things like "It don't cost you a penny to say a few kind words to a person who hasn't had the advantages we had." Grady couldn't for the life of him think of any advantages that had come their way so far.

They didn't talk much for the next couple of hours, just listened to the country-western stations Grady managed to tweak out of the static on the AM radio. They passed a Leaving Ohio, Come Back Soon sign and another one right away that said Entering Pennsylvania, followed by a whole lot of warnings about what would happen if you were picked up for speeding. Not much danger of that in their car, Grady thought.

They were between radio stations, so Lila was humming a happy song. Grady was caught halfway between the excitement of going to a place that might turn out to be the best place yet and the fear that it could be the worst. Not knowing which kept him on edge, but whatever it turned out to be, he knew he could handle it. He had no choice but to make the best of whatever he got.

They hadn't seen a town for quite a while when the engine started to cough, then cut out at the top of a hill.

"Oh, Lordy," Lila said, patting the dashboard. "Don't give up on me now."

"Looks like your friend Russ used cheap tape."

Lila let the car roll as long as gravity kept it moving, then eased it over on the shoulder of the road.

"Go see what the problem is, honey."

Grady got out. He didn't have much faith in his ability to get the car going again, so he looked around for some signs of human life—maybe a farmer who kept an ancient tractor running with chewing gum and toothpicks. There was nothing here but a half-collapsed barn with a faded Mail Pouch Tobacco sign painted on its one vertical wall. Nearby an old chimney stuck up out of a crumbling stone foundation like an exclamation point. A cornfield with streaks of snow left unmelted in the purple shade between the rows stretched out as far as he could see.

Grady sighed and put up the hood, hoping for a sudden flash of genetic mechanical genius. Surely some of that would have been handed down from his father. Grady pulled the tape out of his pocket. He hadn't noticed before, but there were lots of hoses and most of them were taped up. There was a thick layer of black oil over everything.

Lila stuck her head out the window. "You see where it's come loose?"

"I'm checking it out." He wiggled one hose and it popped off, along with the one next to it. They were kind of springy, so he couldn't tell where they had been attached. Which thing was the carburetor? He should've paid more attention to Russ.

By now Lila was out of the car, looking over his shoulder. "We got two hoses loose?"

"Yep."

She leaned in close to the engine. "Well, can you tell where they come from? Because all you need to do is figure that out and tape them back on."

Grady just looked at her.

"Never mind," she said, squeezing his shoulder. "You woulda done that if you could figure it out, wouldn't you, sweetie? I wonder if we've still got the owner's manual in the glove compartment. They usually have little pictures that show how the engine should look."

"Don't matter how the engine should look, Mom. Those people at the commune drove this thing into the ground. It's not moving another inch, unless you got the money to get it towed and more money to get it fixed by somebody who *has* a clue."

"I don't have the money," Lila said. "Leastwise not enough for that."

Grady had figured as much, because when they had stopped at a gas station for lunch, Lila had to feel all around the corners of her purse to find the change to get them one can of Coke to split. He hoped she had a little emergency money tucked away somewhere— enough to get them to the next place. But the only money she made at the commune was from selling her baked goods to the neighbors, and she had to pay back part of that for the stuff she used from the commune kitchen. She couldn't have saved up much.

"Well," Lila said, "let's at least give it one last try. There's two hoses and two places to tape them to. We'll stick them on both ways. One's gotta work."

Grady taped the hoses, then Lila tried to start the car. Nothing. Then he switched the hoses and she tried again. The engine made some grinding noises. Then the grinding slowed down until it stopped. "Battery's dead now," Grady called.

Lila got out of the car and slammed the hood closed. She shaded her eyes from the bright spring sun and looked down the road in both directions. Grady leaned against the car and waited for her to decide what to do next. He sure didn't have any ideas. He marveled at how the brilliant sunshine didn't warm him even the slightest bit.

Lila finally opened the back door and tossed him his backpack.

"What? We're going to walk to New York?"

Lila slammed the door and shouldered her own pack. "Don't be silly. We'll walk until we get help. I'll find somebody. You know I will. I always do."

"But, Mom, we're in the middle of nowhere."

"Every place is somewhere, Grady. If you'd stop running your mouth and start running your feet, we'd be halfway there by now."

"Halfway where?"

"Anywhere!" she shouted over her shoulder. She didn't even look to see if Grady was following. She knew he would.

He always did.

CHAPTER 3

About an hour later, Grady was so cold his toes were numb. "Why couldn't we be doing this in June instead of April?"

"Because now is when we needed to leave," Lila said. "Anyways, I think I see a town up ahead."

She was right. There was a building. Didn't look like much, but Grady was ready to take anything with four walls and a roof. Heck, even three walls and a roof.

As they got closer to it, Grady's heart dropped. "It's only another old barn!"

"But look, Grady. There's something beyond. I think we're coming to a town."

Some town. There was a sign that said Welcome to Bedelia followed by four houses, a gas station, and a restaurant with a beat-up old trailer out back.

"Now isn't that lucky." Lila pulled herself up tall. "This town can provide me a position in an occupation with which I am already familiar."

When Lila was nervous, she started talking what she described as "fancy, like one of them college professors" to impress people. Grady hated when she did that. Sometimes when he could see people laughing behind Lila's back, he would glare at them until they got the message that it wasn't okay to make fun of her. Grady knew that Lila was smart in ways that didn't show on the outside. Phony talk kept people from seeing her the way she really was.

Lila stopped Grady at the door of the restaurant so she could comb through his hair and her own with her fingers before they went in. Her red wavy hair fell into place, while his straight brown hair slid right back over his forehead the second her fingers left it. He had his father's hair—"that slippery Flood hair," Lila called it.

When they went inside the restaurant, the first thing that hit Grady in the face was heat, which was surely welcome. That was followed by the smell of grease that had fried a few too many fish. He was so hungry, it made his mouth water.

The waitress behind the counter smiled as they entered. She was old, real old, but she had bright red lipstick and bright blue eye shadow. With her fish-white skin, Grady thought she looked like a greeting card for the Fourth of July. The name June was embroidered on her uniform pocket. "Sit yourselves down, folks. You took me by surprise. I didn't hear your car pull up."

Grady hitched himself onto one of the twirly stools, but Lila remained standing and reached out to shake June's hand. "Well, funny you should mention that, because that is a part of the predicament me and my offspring here, Grady, seem to find ourselves in. My name is Lila Flood, and my vee-hicle appears to have underwent some sort of a misfortunate occurrence."

Grady tried to shrink down into his jacket so the collar muffled the syrupy falseness of her voice.

The waitress leaned closer to Lila and squinted. "I'm sorry, dearie, but I can't make head nor tail of what you're trying to tell me."

Before June could mock her, Grady jumped in with, "Our car broke down. It's a piece of crap."

Lila gave him a look, then dialed her smile up a notch. "Please excuse my son's couthless behavior."

June laughed. "Not a problem, darlin'. I've heard much worse from the truck drivers passing through, believe me. Now, you're lucky to have landed here, because Sal Palvino across the street is probably the best mechanic for miles around. I'll give him a call and he can tow your car to his gas station. What's it look like?"

"It's mostly duct tape," Grady said. "The rest is rust."

June smiled and waggled a shiny red fingernail at Grady. "I like your sense of humor, kid." She reached for the phone on the wall.

Grady searched June's face for any sign of mockery, then relaxed a little. It was clear that June wasn't making fun of his mother. There wouldn't be any need to give her one of his dark looks.

"Wait, June," Lila said. "I can't have the car fixed. Leastwise not right now. I gotta work awhile first. Save up some, you know?" Lila was talking like her normal self now, and June seemed nice—the kind of person who might be able to help them. On a scale of one to ten, this place was already up to a five.

June put the phone back on the hook. "Okay. I catch your drift. You got somethin' lined up, honey?"

"Well, we're headed for New York."

June raised her eyebrows. They were just drawn in black pencil, no hairs. "You got yourself a job in the Big Apple?"

"No. We're going to the state. Not the city."

"Well, that's good, too, sweetie, but you're at least fifty miles from the New York State line. How are you getting to New York with no car?"

Lila sat down at the counter. "That's the problem. I was hoping maybe you might have something for me here. I'm a good waitress and a hard worker. I got experience and all."

Grady twirled his seat so his back was to them and turtled his neck down into the collar. This was the part he hated most, when Lila had to beg for a job. Not that she wasn't good at it, because she always got work. But it made him feel crummy all the same, as if they weren't as good as other folks.

"Look," June said. "I'd give you a job if I could, but you can see we're not exactly runnin' over with customers here. Ever since they opened up the new section of the turnpike, all we get are the people who are too cheap to pay the toll."

Yeah, well, that would be us, Grady thought. No way Lila would spend good money to drive on any darn road.

Lila stood and shouldered her backpack. "Don't you trouble yourself none about us, June. Thanks anyway. Sorry to have bothered you. C'mon, Grady. We gotta get going."

Grady must have shown the sudden panic he felt, because June caught Lila's sleeve. "No, wait, honey. We'll think of something. Sit down and have a bite to eat. We'll figure this out."

Lila turned around and slid in beside Grady. "I want you to know I don't take no charity. I work for my keep."

"Don't worry about it. The meat loaf and mashed potatoes haven't been too popular today. You'd be doing us a favor if you'd take them off our hands. Mashed potatoes don't keep, and the meat loaf was from Sunday."

"I guess we could do that," Lila said. "I mean if you were going to throw it out."

June disappeared into the kitchen and came back with two plates of food. Grady almost swallowed that hunk of meat loaf without chewing. It was that good. Or he was that hungry.

June poured Grady a glass of milk, then coffee for Lila and herself. "You think you might have enough money for bus tickets? There's no bus going through here, but I could give you a lift over to the station at Addieville. Depending on where you're going in New York, it probably wouldn't be more than forty dollars for you, maybe fifteen, twenty for the kid." She looked at Grady. "You're not twelve yet, are you?"

Grady's mouth was full, so he nodded.

June shrugged. "That's all right. You'll slouch a little. So we're talking fifty-five, maybe sixty. You got that much, dearie?"

Lila held her coffee cup in both hands, hunching as if she were warming herself over a campfire. "No, not that much. Not even close."

"Well, if I had it, I'd loan it to you myself. I'm always doing darn fool things like that. If I had every dime I ever loaned to a complete stranger with a good story, I'd be a rich woman."

"That's the Lord's own truth." An old guy with a grease-stained apron had come out of the kitchen.

June tilted her head toward him. "That's Bob, my husband. You been eavesdropping on Lila and me?"

He switched the toothpick he was chewing to the opposite corner of his mouth. "Don't I always? How else would I keep those truckers from running off with my beautiful wife?" He smiled, leaving the tooth-pick balanced on his bottom teeth.

"So you got any ideas?" June asked.

Bob leaned on the counter in front of Lila. "You need to have a car where you're going?"

"Well, I'm used to having my car"—Lila bit her lip and thought for a minute—"but I guess I could manage without it. Depends on where we end up."

"Maybe Sal would buy it, then," Bob said. "That would give you the money for bus tickets."

June patted him on the head. "Bob, you may look dumb as a doorknob, but your poor old brain is still breathing in there." She grabbed the phone and punched in the numbers. "Sal? June. I got a customer here. . . . Yeah, yeah, very funny . . . I got a customer here who might want to sell her car. . . . No, she can't bring it in. It's stalled down the road." She turned to Lila. "Which direction?"

Lila pointed.

"Out toward Hester. Can't be too far. They walked in from there. Okay, thanks, Sal. Stop by after you take a look-see. I got some peach pie left." She laughed. "You know it, baby. Thanks!" She hung up the phone. "He's going right now to check it out. He'll give you a fair price."

June cut two big pieces of peach pie.

Lila pushed the plate away. "I can't let you give us that, June. There's no way you were throwing out that pie."

What was she doing? Grady hadn't had a piece of pie for months. He hunkered down and curved his arm around his plate so Lila couldn't get at it.

June winked at Grady and pushed Lila's plate back at her. "You can't have a meal without something sweet at the end, Lila. It's a rule around here."

Lila picked up her fork. "Well, I wouldn't want to go breaking rules, but I'll do some work for you in return."

Grady took a big bite of the pie. It had a crust so flaky it practically fell apart when he touched it with his fork. Man, he never tasted anything like it. When he finished the pie, Grady licked his finger and used it to pick up every last little flake of crust on the plate.

June poured Grady some more milk. "You liked that, did you, Grady?"

"Yes, ma'am. That's about the best pie I ever tasted."

"Don't be telling her that," Bob said. "She'll want me to pay her more money."

Lila was already working without June telling her what to do. First she swept the floor. Then she gathered up all the napkin holders and filled them from the big pack of napkins behind the counter.

Grady finished his second glass of milk, then ducked out to use the restroom behind the building before Lila got the idea of him working for his pie, too.

Before he went back in, Grady looked around to see if maybe he had missed seeing part of the town before. He hadn't. There was nothing here. Even Sunward Path had more buildings than this place. June and Bob should move their restaurant to a bigger town if they didn't want to be throwing out their meat loaf every day. Anybody could see there weren't enough customers here to keep the place in business. Not a car or truck coming or going as far as the eye could see.

So there was no work for Lila here, and Grady couldn't see what good it would do to take a bus into New York. What if they used up all their money on the bus fare and didn't find work there, either? He wished Lila would worry more about things like that so it didn't all fall on his shoulders.

By the time Grady got back inside, Lila was laughing and carrying on with Bob and June as if they'd all gone to high school together, even though Bob and June were about a hundred years older than her. Lila was finishing up filling the sugar bowls when the door opened and a guy came in. He was tall and good looking with dark hair that hung over one eyebrow like Elvis Presley. He should've had the word *trouble* tattooed across his forehead. "Hey, Sal," June said. "Take a load off your feet and tell us what you think of the car."

Sal slid onto the stool next to Lila and gave her a grin. Grady got a prickly feeling on the back of his neck. So here was the next Russ. And they weren't even in New York yet.

CHAPTER
4

June poured Sal a cup of coffee. He put four spoons of sugar in it. Grady was almost hypnotized watching him stir. Sal finally put down the spoon and looked up at Lila, smiling to show off his movie star teeth. He even had a dimple in one cheek. Why did they have to keep running into guys like this? "I have one question for you," Sal said. "What did you do with the horse?"

"What horse?" Lila asked.

"The horse you used to tow that car, because there's no way that heap got here on its own. Whoever worked on it last was clueless."

"It got here just fine," Grady said. Oh, great. Now he was defending Russ's mechanical skills to the new Russ.

"Look, kid. I'm not trying to insult your car. It's a miracle that you got here, that's all."

"So you can't give me any money for it?" Lila asked. "I was hoping for enough to get bus tickets to New York."

Sal tried to sip the coffee, but it was too hot. He wiped his mouth with the back of his hand. "Sorry, but I'd have to spend a fortune to repair that car, and then there's no guarantee I could actually get it running again. I don't have any use for a car I can't fix. Besides, it's got too much rust on it. Nobody would pay me enough money for it to cover the parts."

"Can't you use some of the good parts, Sal?" June slid a piece of pie across the counter to him. "Couldn't you pull about seventy, eighty bucks' worth of stuff off it?"

"June, I'd like to help you out, but the whole thing's held together with duct tape. There's not a decent part to be had."

"That's okay," Lila said. "If you can't, you can't. Thanks for looking at it, though."

Sal ducked his head and smiled. "My pleasure." Then he looked at Lila from under that lock of Elvis hair. The *trouble* tattoo had turned into a flashing neon sign.

Suddenly June smacked herself on the head. "Why didn't I think of this before? Roger and Ethel Fernwald were in here for dinner the other night. They're moving to Florida and they want to find someone to take care of Roger's dad, Charlie. He won't sell the farm, but they're afraid to have him living out there all alone."

Bob laughed. "Hoo, boy! Old Charlie Fernwald? Did he agree to having a babysitter?"

"I don't think he has anything to say about it. Roger is doing the hiring. Charlie does get to pick the person, though."

"Isn't Charlie Fernwald that crazy old guy up on Wheeler Hill?" Sal asked.

June piled the dishes and put them in the sink. "He's not crazy. Maybe a little—what do they call it? Eccentric." She turned back to Lila. "What do you think, honey? There's a nice little cottage on the farm for the caretaker."

Lila perked right up at that. "Really? We'd have our own house?"

Grady knew those were magic words. He and Lila hadn't lived in their own house since the accident. Lila's dream was to have a real home again. He'd never get her away from here if they got their own place.

"You'd get all your meals, too," June said, "and

some pay. You'd have to do the cleaning and cooking, laundry and such, if I remember right. You could do it until you had the money to move on. I wouldn't tell Roger that, though. He wants somebody permanent. But with Charlie Fernwald, nobody's likely to last more than a month or so."

"Well, there's really no reason we have to go to New York right away," Lila said. "Sometimes a good opportunity just drops into your lap. Right, Grady?"

He avoided looking at his mother. He knew she'd have that old "see, I told you" look on her face.

Bob wiped the counter with a wet rag. "If I was you, I'd meet old Charlie Fernwald before I started making any plans, because he's not exactly what I'd call a good opportunity. You'll have your hands full with that one."

"Well, I don't want to go bragging' on myself," Lila said, "but I have a way with people. I bet that old gentleman and me will get along fine. How can I get to meet him?"

Sal stood up. "I'll take you out there, Lila. I have a kid watching the station for me."

"Hey, hold on a minute," June said. "Charlie don't

like surprises. Let me give him a call and ask if you can come over."

"Why give him a chance to say no?" Sal said. "We'll head out right now." He helped Lila on with her jacket, and they started for the door. Grady picked up the backpacks and followed. Why was this guy in such an all-fired hurry?

"I'm going to call Roger, too," June said. "He can meet you there. Might smooth things over a bit."

When they got to his pickup truck, Sal looked surprised to see Grady. "Oh, yeah, kid. Sorry. You can go, too." He took the backpacks from Grady and tossed them into the truck bed. Lila started to get in, but Grady squeezed ahead and plunked himself in the middle of the seat—right between his mother and trouble.

———————————

A few miles down the road, they went through a town. It wasn't much, but at least it had some stores, a couple of churches, and a bunch of houses. Grady had his eye out for a library but didn't see one. Of course it could have been hidden down a side street.

Sal drove past an empty parking lot with a big school

building. Grady read a sign that said Melvin Proctor Junior-Senior High School and felt his meat loaf roll around in his stomach.

"The school looks closed," Lila said. "Is this some sort of holiday?"

"It's closed for good," Sal said. "Now they bus all the kids from seventh grade up over to Addieville. It's a big central school."

School was the worst part of moving to a new place. The first day he stepped into a new school, it was like diving into a tank of freezing water. Grady wondered what names he'd be called here. Maybe he'd be lucky this time. Maybe he'd dive into that tank of water and drown right then and there. Or maybe he'd be even luckier and they'd move on before anybody tried to make him go to school.

"Grady?" Lila had been saying something to him. "Huh?"

"Sal says there's a nice big central school here."

"That's great, Mom." Maybe if it was big, he could be invisible. Although he had been in big schools before. Nobody ever had any trouble figuring out that he was the weird new kid and zeroing in on him.

"You should see the gym in that place," Sal said.

"They have the best ath-a-letic program in ten counties. People from all around here go to the games, whether they got kids or not. What are you in, kid, about seventh grade?"

Grady nodded, not that it was any of Sal's business.

"Well, then you could play junior varsity baseball. The season just started a few weeks ago. Addieville's team came in second in state regionals last year."

Great. There was nothing Grady hated more than going to school with a bunch of jocks. At least on the communes all the kids were oddballs and you could score points by being good at folk dancing or weaving cane chair seats.

Sal gunned the engine as they started up a steep hill. "That's Charlie Fernwald's place up there."

There was a big old farmhouse, a couple of barns, and what looked like a kids' playhouse off under some trees. There were no other houses in sight. As they pulled into the long driveway, an old man came down off the porch. The way he was marching toward them, Grady was sure he was coming to run them off his property.

They barely got out of the truck before the old guy started in. "You the folks June called about?"

"Yes, sir," Lila said with her biggest smile. She held out her hand. "I'm Lila Flood, and I'm delighted to be applying for the position of being your personal assistant. My spe-shee-ality is making a gracious and healthifying home for those of the elder persuasion." When Charlie didn't shake her hand, Lila let hers fall to her side, but her smile got even brighter and phonier.

Grady groaned inside at Lila's fancy language.

It was pretty obvious that Mr. Charlie Fernwald wasn't impressed one single bit by Lila's act. "Whatever it is you do, young lady, I'm sure you're real good at it. But you're just not going to do it here, because I have not as yet been persuaded to be elder. So if you'll all climb back into that truck, I have things to do."

He turned and started walking away. That's when Lila caught sight of the small house. Now that they were close up, Grady could see that it wasn't a kids' playhouse. It was a real cottage. It even had a front porch with two rocking chairs. Lila had a thing for porches. "Oh, Grady, look," she whispered. "There's the little house. Isn't that the cutest thing you ever saw?"

"Mom, the guy doesn't want us here."

Lila lifted her chin. "Oh, he will, Grady. You wait.

He will." She ran after Charlie Fernwald and caught up to him on the porch of the big house. Grady followed slowly. He wanted to be nearby in case Charlie was mean to Lila. Sal didn't seem to care about that. He leaned against the side of the truck and lit a cigarette.

As Grady got closer, he heard Lila say, "If you would give me a chance to demonstrate my kitchen skills, Mr. Fernwald, I'm sure you would discover that I'm an excellent chef."

"I'm sure you are, but I've been feeding myself ever since my wife died, which is four years now. I don't look like I'm starving, do I?"

He sure didn't. There was definite evidence of a potbelly under his farmer's overalls. He was mostly bald on top with a fringe of hair over his ears, but he looked pretty strong for an old guy. He had freckles on his face and all the way over his bald head. His hair hadn't turned gray or white the way most old geezers' did. It looked like red hair that had faded, like an old blanket that had been washed so many times, most of the color had come out of it.

Charlie finally noticed Grady. "Is this your kid?"

"Yes, sir. This is my offspring, Grady."

Lila nudged Grady, so he held out his hand and Charlie shook it.

"Well, nice to meet you both, but even if I wanted help here—which I definitely don't—there's no room for two people in that cottage. It's barely big enough for one."

"Oh, Grady and me is used to fitting in small places," Lila said. "We've never had nothing so nice as this." She put her hand to her mouth, realizing she had dropped her fancy talk and given away the fact that they were nobody special.

Charlie lifted his chin so he could look at them through the bottom part of his glasses. "All right, what's your deal? You're not one of those aides Roger keeps sending out from the agency, because June at the restaurant is the one who called me. So you're just passing through here? Is that it?"

"We would have passed through if our car hadn't died," Grady said.

Charlie shaded his eyes to see Sal standing by the truck. "Now this is starting to make some sense. That's the guy with the gas station out by June's place. You just need a place to stay while the car is being fixed?"

"Oh, no," Lila said. "I'm looking for a permanent position."

That's when Grady thought he got the picture.

Charlie didn't want a permanent person. He just needed to look like he had one until his son moved away. Grady decided to use the honest approach, since Lila's professor act hadn't worked. "Mom needs to earn enough to get a new car. Well, not a new one. A used one that runs good. Then we'll be moving on. So we won't be around here all that long."

Lila gave Grady a poke in the ribs, but he could tell by the change in Charlie's expression that he was on the right track. Besides, he and Lila had to have somewhere to live until they could get out of there, and he was pretty sure Sal might be offering to have them bunk in with him. No way Grady was going to let that happen.

Charlie rubbed his chin. "This might not be so bad. My son and his wife are moving in two weeks. Long as they think I have somebody, they'll leave me alone. You could stay here until you had enough money for the car. By then Roger would be long gone."

"But you would let me cook and clean for you, wouldn't you?" Lila asked. "I wouldn't feel right about taking money for doing nothing. I don't ever take no charity."

Charlie didn't get a chance to answer, because a car came into the driveway so fast it was spitting gravel behind it. "Here's my son now. Let me handle this. We'll work things out after he leaves."

A guy got out of the car and ran toward the house. "Don't make any snap judgments, Dad," he called out. "Let's talk this over."

"There's nothing to talk over, Roger."

Roger bounded up onto the porch. "But, Dad, you've turned down so many applicants."

"I know. That's why I'm hiring this woman."

Lila gave a little gasp and squeezed Grady's hand.

"Well, now, that's wonderful." Roger turned and gave Lila and Grady a once-over. "Does she have any references?"

Grady folded his arms to hide the ripped cuff on his jacket.

"You think I've taken leave of my senses?" Charlie asked. "You think I'm going to hire some complete stranger who drops in out of nowhere without checking on her references?"

"Well, no, of course not, Dad. I didn't mean to imply . . ."

"Just remember I've given you every bit of common

sense you have, Roger. Many's the time I've saved you from being bamboozled by some con artist over the years. Isn't that right?"

Roger looked like a scolded puppy. He mumbled something Grady couldn't hear.

Charlie turned to Lila. "Now, when did you say you could start?"

Lila clapped. Grady hoped she wouldn't go into her happy dance and blow the whole deal. "I can start this very minute."

Roger looked a bit uneasy, but smiled and patted his father on the back. "Well, then, I guess it's settled, Dad."

Grady left them to work out the arrangements. He ran down the driveway and pulled their backpacks out of the truck bed.

Sal ground out the cigarette with the heel of his boot. "So she got the job?"

"Yep."

He looked past Grady at Lila. "Guess I'll be seeing a lot of you folks from now on." That neon sign was flashing like a beacon.

"I don't think so," Grady said. "The old goat says we can't have anybody come around here. Says he chases people off with a gun. I'd stay away if I was you."

As Grady lugged their backpacks up to the house, he could hear the truck spin its wheels going out of the driveway.

Good-bye, Russ number two.

CHAPTER

5

Grady waited on the porch of the little house for Lila to come back. He tried to peek inside, but there were curtains pulled shut across the windows. The whole house was only half the size of a small trailer. Grady put down the backpacks and sat in one of the rocking chairs. The cottage was right at the top of a hill. Grady could see for a long distance, but there was nothing much to look at. The only signs of life were barns with silos and a small herd of cows dotting the distant landscape. For once Grady hoped Lila would get fed up with her job quick, because it didn't look as if there was much to hang around for. If she could earn them enough money to get a set of wheels, they could move on to someplace more exciting.

Charlie's old farmhouse was white with green shutters. Behind it was a big red barn with a silo. If there were snow on the ground, it would look almost exactly like the country Christmas card Lila always taped to the wall over her bed when they moved to a new place. Grady had once asked her if it reminded her of home. She told him it looked like the place she'd like to live someday. And now here it was in real life, in plain view from her front porch. Grady could have a hard time getting her to leave here.

The only things that caught Grady's interest were the three tall TV antennas in the big open yard in front of Charlie's porch. At least they should get some pretty good reception with all that fancy equipment. Maybe life on Charlie's farm wouldn't be totally boring after all. There sure hadn't been any TV on the commune. No radio, either.

A couple of car doors slammed, then Charlie's son and his wife drove past the cottage. Grady could see Lila and Charlie heading his way. Lila looked like a little kid all set to open a big pile of birthday presents. If she walked any bouncier, she'd be skipping.

Charlie Fernwald pulled some keys out of his pocket as they came up on the porch. "This one is for the front door. The smaller one is for the back. You don't need to use them, though. Around here we leave things unlocked, unless you're hiding some diamonds in those backpacks."

"Oh, no," Lila said. "I don't have nothing like diamonds. Only the one little rhinestone tennis bracelet I got from the five-and-dime is all, and I got that on clearance. I never played tennis, but I thought the bracelet was pretty."

Grady wished Lila could tell when somebody was making a joke. He saw Charlie shake his head and smile. Grady glared at him so he'd know it wasn't okay to make fun of her.

The door stuck at first, but Charlie pounded it with his fist and it opened. Grady followed them inside, dragging the backpacks. It was one small room with two doors and another doorway covered by a curtain. He could see that the one led outside in the back. He couldn't figure out what the other two were until Charlie opened one. "Here's your bathroom. There's no tub, but the shower works." He pulled back the curtain. "This is a good-sized closet." Charlie eyed their pitiful pile of belongings. "If you don't have too much to store, you could put a cot in here and call it a second bedroom." He pulled a string to turn on the bare lightbulb that hung from the ceiling.

Grady leaned past him and looked inside. A cot would fill that room from wall to wall. The swinging light made the little red flowers on the peeling wallpaper look like ladybugs crawling across the walls. "Where's the first bedroom?" Grady asked.

"Right here." Charlie walked across the room and grabbed a handle on the wall. A bed pulled down, barely clearing the old couch and stuffed chair. They all had to squeeze against the wall to make room for it. "Murphy bed," Charlie explained. "Pulls up out of the way when you don't need it." He lifted it back in place and went over to a corner where there was a small stove, refrigerator, and sink. Charlie tugged another handle and a piece of the wall pivoted up to become a table, its legs folding out from somewhere underneath. The table filled about half of the room.

"What if one of us wants to eat and the other one wants to sleep at the same time?" Grady asked.

"Guess you'd be out of luck," Charlie said. "I told you it was small. I built it as a playhouse when our kids were little. Then my wife had me add the bed and kitchen so it could be a guesthouse. If you don't think it's big enough, you can be on your way."

"Oh, it's plenty of room," Lila said. "We'll manage fine here, Mr. Fernwald. Don't you worry none about that."

"All right, then. If you send the boy up to the house, I'll get the cot out for him."

"My name is Grady." If Lila had been paying attention, Grady would have felt her elbow in his ribs for that remark. She was running her fingers over the table with a dreamy look in her eyes.

Charlie stopped at the door and turned to look at Grady. "Fair enough. Grady. That your first name or your last name?"

"First name."

He nodded. "Funny, you don't run into any Bobs, Bills, or Marys anymore. Seems like everybody's got to be a Cody or a Crosby or a Madison. Kids today have their names on backwards, if you ask me."

"Nobody asked you," Grady mumbled.

"What's that?"

"I said I'll come right after you. To the house, I mean. For the cot."

Charlie's eyes narrowed. "Uh-huh. Give me about

fifteen minutes to find it. I'll leave it out on the porch for you."

When Charlie let the screen door slam behind him, Lila woke up from her daydream and ran out onto the porch. "Oh, Mr. Fernwald, what time do you want me to come up and cook your dinner?"

"I don't need anybody cooking for me. I have a whole freezer full of dinners. Salisbury steak with french fries. Have it twice a day. Some days three times, if I run out of Sugar Loops."

Lila kicked into high gear with her healthy food speech—propaganda from their first commune. "But that's not good for you, Mr. Fernwald. You should have some nice fresh vegetables. Maybe a salad."

Charlie Fernwald came back and took hold of the porch railing. "Look, Lisa, I'm sure you mean well."

"Lila," Grady corrected.

Charlie cleared his throat. "Lila. I'm going to tell it to you real nice and clear. My mama died over forty years ago and I haven't eaten a vegetable since. Even my dear departed wife couldn't make me eat any rabbit food, so forget about it. I'll see you in the morning."

Lila came back into the house and dropped down on the couch. A little cloud of dust came out of it when she landed. "Grady, I do believe I was sent here for a purpose. It wasn't no accident, that car breaking down where it did."

"Of course it wasn't no accident," Grady said. "Russ made it happen because he's an idiot. Any fool knows a car won't run on duct tape."

"No, really. Come here and listen to me." She patted the cushion next to her, raising up another puff of dust. "Grady, I'm having a vision clear as anything."

Lila was always having visions. She was always seeing into the future, only the future she was seeing was never anything like the future that really happened. "Grady, I have been sent here to save that man."

"Save who? Charlie Fernwald?"

"Yes. That man is killing himself with all that bad food he's eating, and I'm going to rescue him."

"How can he be killing himself? He's got to be about a hundred years old. Besides, anybody that mean will live forever, even if he don't eat nothing but pork rinds dipped in hog grease."

All the talk about food was making Grady hungry. He got up to check out the fridge. It was empty except for a box of baking soda, which didn't look like anything you'd want to eat. He opened all the little cupboards over the sink. There were some dishes and glasses and a couple of pots and pans. No food. "What are we supposed to eat here? Maybe the old geezer is all set with his frozen stuff, but there's nothing for us. I'll ask him if we can have a couple of those sauce-berry steak things."

"You won't ask any such thing, Grady. We had a good lunch. We don't need no more than one big meal a day. I'm still full."

"Well, I'm not! Jeez, Mom, you're always bugging me about how a growing boy has to have his three squares a day. What happened to *that* rule all of a sudden?"

"I'm sure we'll get this all straightened out in the morning. I don't want to give that man no reason to send us away before I even get a chance to work my magic on him."

"Magic! How about waving your magic wand and giving your son a meal before he starves to death?"

"You'll live, Grady. Make yourself useful and run on up to the house to get that cot. Otherwise you'll be sleeping on the floor tonight. Then you'll have something to complain about."

"I got another thing to complain about. That guy has all those TV antennas outside, but do you see a TV in here? Would it kill him to give us one tiny TV?"

"What's got into you? We never had a TV, except for that room over the restaurant. Seems to me you can manage perfectly well without a TV."

"Fine!" Grady slammed out the door and headed for the big house. He found the cot on the porch, but he didn't stop there. Through the front window he could see Charlie Fernwald sitting on his couch, eating a dinner out of a little cardboard box with a plastic spoon. He knocked on the door.

It took Charlie a few minutes to get up and come over. "Didn't you see the cot? I put it over by the steps. There's a pile of bedding next to it. Let me know if you need an extra quilt. I got plenty."

"You should let my mother make meals for you," Grady said. "She's a great cook."

"I'm sure she is, but I don't need a cook. You can stay in the house, though. Long as you keep out of my hair, I don't care what you do. All I ask is that you leave the place the way you found it. "

He started to close the door, but Grady stuck out his

foot to block it. "Hey, wait a minute. We got another problem here. Meals were supposed to come with this job. If Mom doesn't cook for you, how do we get anything to eat?"

Charlie rubbed his forehead. "Hadn't thought about that. All right." He dug around in the pocket of his overalls and pulled out a wrinkled twenty-dollar bill. "Here, take this and get some food for yourselves."

"Where's the grocery store?"

"Where do you think it would be? Down in town."

"Well, how are we supposed to get there? We don't have a car, and it's too far to walk." Grady was afraid Charlie would say he had to walk twice as far when he was a kid. That's what old people always did— brag about how much harder they had it when they were kids, walking through blizzards up mountains to school. Who did they think they were fooling? No way any kid would work *that* hard to get to school.

Charlie held out some keys, but he hung on to them a little too tight for Grady to take them. "Is your mother a good driver?"

"She is when she's not trying to drive some piece of junk."

Charlie looked at him hard, then let go of the keys. "I must be crazy, because I don't know either one of you from Adam, but I can't let you starve. My truck is in the barn. Go get what you need from town. I'm calling Sheriff Halloren so he knows it's all right for you to be driving the truck."

Charlie caught Grady's arm as he started for the door. "The sheriff is a good friend of mine, so don't get any ideas about leaving town. He'll have his eye out for you one way or the other."

Grady wanted to throw the keys back in his face, but he was too hungry to go without dinner. It made him mad that every time they started in a new place, people treated them like bums. Lila always said that being honest was the most important thing in the world. But what good did it do to be honest when everybody expected you to lie and steal? Grady wanted to run off with Charlie Fernwald's truck and leave it in a junkyard a hundred miles away. He could do it, too. He had learned to drive a tractor on their first commune when he was seven and had been driving anything he could get his hands on ever since.

If he did steal the truck, Grady knew he would be

getting Lila into trouble as much as himself. He'd have to be satisfied with just picturing old Charlie red faced and sputtering. Grady wished he could really do it, though. It would serve Charlie right for not trusting them.

CHAPTER
6

Grady could tell that his mother was spending most of the twenty dollars on stuff she wanted to cook for Charlie. "Hey, that was supposed to be for our food. Besides, the old coot doesn't even want you to cook for him."

Lila examined nine zucchinis before she found the three she wanted and put them in her basket. "That's what he thinks now, but I'm going to turn his thinking clear around. You just wait and see."

"Well, you're not going to turn him around with zucchini squashes, that's for sure." Right away Grady wished he hadn't said that. Why couldn't he just keep his mouth shut and let her have her little dreams? It didn't take much to make Lila happy.

Grady left his mother sorting through the carrots

and wandered around the store until he came to the toy aisle. It was the usual junk—crummy plastic stuff sealed to little cards with more plastic. He used to beg for toys like these when he was younger, thinking each one was a little treasure just waiting for him to open it. Funny how you see things different when you grow up. The only thing that looked even halfway interesting to him now was a plastic slingshot, but he could tell it would probably break on the first try. He held it up, card and all, and pretended to be taking aim at one of the ceiling lights. Right away a pimply-faced kid wearing a big red Hokey Pokey Grocery pin stopped piling up boxes of diapers and came toward him.

"You gonna buy that? Because if you're not, you'd better put it down right now or else."

Grady tried to figure out how old he was. Sixteen, maybe seventeen at the most. "Or else what?"

The guy didn't have an answer for that.

"Look, Hokey," Grady said, "I don't want to buy this thing, but I might be interested in renting it. How much would it be to rent it overnight? Maybe two nights?"

The kid jutted out his chin. "Oh, a smart guy,

huh? Well, for your information, Hokey Pokey is the name of the store. And we don't do rentals."

"You ought to bring it up with the manager."

"I am the manager. Front end manager, four-thirty to midnight."

This guy had just handed Grady such a great straight line, he was tempted to go into a string of one-liners about what a rear end manager might do. But Grady figured this guy didn't have a sense of humor and there was nobody nearby to hear the jokes. No fun in that. Besides, Grady was so hungry his stomach had gone beyond growling and was moving up to barking. He put the slingshot back on its hook and went to find Lila.

She was checking out with a bunch of veggies and some baking stuff. "What's for dinner?" Grady asked.

Lila pulled two jars out of her cart. Peanut butter and jam. Not the good kinds, either. Hokey Pokey brand. And a loaf of bread that had *day old* scrawled across the wrapper in purple marker. Grady gave the loaf a squeeze. That *day old* must have been written on there a week ago.

Grady didn't try to hide his disappointment. It

wasn't fair. That money was supposed to be for their food, not Charlie's. Lila reached over and rubbed Grady's back. "You and me can make do for a few days, Grady. Just till we're settled in for good."

Grady nodded. It wasn't the first time they'd had to "make do," and he'd eaten lots worse than stale peanut butter sandwiches. He wasn't going to bust Lila's bubble again.

One of the lights in the parking lot was broken, so Grady almost ran their cart into a guy who was standing by a car having a smoke. Lila had parked Charlie's truck under the other light, so it was easy to find, not that the lot was all that big. As Lila pulled out onto the road, Grady opened the lid of the peanut butter jar and scooped his finger into it. Not bad. It might be a cheapo brand, but at least it was chunky.

Lila glanced over. "Don't you be eating in this truck."

"Why not?"

"This here's practically a new truck, Grady. Can't be more'n four, maybe five years old. Still has a little new car smell to it. Least it did before you opened that jar."

Grady thought it smelled more like old Charlie

than new car. He was busy fishing for another finger-ful of peanut butter, so he didn't say anything.

Lila saw him in the light of a passing neon sign. "You in that jar again? Can't you wait till we get home?"

"Mom, I'm half starved!"

She sighed. "All right, but don't be getting none of that peanut grease on these seats or I'll give you what for when we get home. Charlie has trusted his truck with me, and it's going back in the same shape I took it out."

Lila was always threatening to give him "what for." One time Grady had asked her what "what for" was, and she said he didn't want to find out. So far he hadn't.

They were about halfway back to Charlie's when Lila put her hand on Grady's arm. The rearview mirror made a band of light across her eyes. "I don't want you to be scared or nothing, but I think somebody is following us. Can you see who it is?"

Grady closed the jar and turned around in his seat. "All I can see is headlights, Mom. Just keep going. We can't be that far from Charlie's."

"Did you see that weird guy in the parking lot?" Lila asked. "It's not him, is it? He was watching us all the way back to the truck."

Grady wanted to tell her that wasn't a big deal. Guys were always watching her on account of how pretty she was. But he didn't think that would calm her down any. "It's prob'ly nothing, Mom, but if it bothers you, speed up a little so we lose him."

Lila gave the truck some more gas and leaned close to the steering wheel, squinting at the road ahead. "I wish I knew these parts better. Hard to see where we are. Is he still coming after us, Grady? I don't dare look back."

Grady knelt on the seat backward. "He's right behind us."

Lila sped up some more, but so did the other car. Grady was beginning to think she was right. That guy really was following them. Probably thought a small woman and a skinny kid were fair game. But Grady knew his mother was a lot stronger than she looked and so was he. He felt around behind the seat to see if Charlie kept a tire iron there, but all he found was some spare change. All of a sudden he saw the big Fernwald Farm sign at the end of Charlie's driveway. "Hey, Mom! We missed it! We just passed Charlie's place!"

"You sure?"

"Yeah. I saw the sign."

"That guy still behind us?"

"Yep. Right on our tail."

"All right. I got to find a place to turn around. This road ain't wide enough for a U-turn. You keep your eyes peeled for a driveway."

All of a sudden the dashboard glowed red for a second, then again. Grady looked in the side mirror and saw flashing red lights behind them.

"Oh, jeez! Mom, you gotta stop!"

"I'm not stopping till I get us home safe."

"But Mom, it's a cop!"

"Just because someone has a flashing red light on his car don't make him no cop, Grady. They have catalogs where you can order flashing lights and sirens for your car and badges and everything. I just heard on the radio the other day about a man who fooled people into thinking he was a cop with that stuff. Then you know what he did? He murdered them."

The red lights were next to them now as the car passed them.

"They don't have Morgan County Sheriff cars in no catalog, Mom."

The sheriff's car had slowed ahead of them, blocking the road.

"I see your point, Grady," Lila said, and she pulled Charlie's truck over to the shoulder.

It took a long time for the sheriff to come back to their car. Lila had pulled about fifty things out of her purse before she found her driver's license, but she had it ready and the window rolled down by the time he got to them.

"I'm sorry, Officer. Was I goin' over the speed limit? I thought you were some weirdo pursuing me and my offspring, Grady, here. I'm not familiarized with these roads on account of I'm new to these parts."

"You may be new around here," the sheriff said, "but this truck isn't."

"That's exactly right," Lila said, giving the sheriff a big smile. "This here truck belongs to Mr. Charlie Fernwald, for which I've been hired to be a personal dietitian. I was in town getting the food for his meals tomorrow and I missed seeing his driveway back there."

The sheriff touched the wide brim of his hat. "I thought that might be your problem. There's a farm with a circle driveway up ahead. Follow me and I'll flash the red lights again when we approach Charlie's driveway."

"That's real nice of you, Officer. Thanks."

Lila followed the sheriff's car down the road to the turnaround. "Isn't he the sweetest thing? Can you imagine he knew Charlie's truck? Must be a real friendly town if everybody knows each other that well. We were lucky he happened to come along."

"He didn't just happen to come along, Mom. Charlie said he was going to call the sheriff to check up on us. He was afraid we'd run off with his truck."

"Why, I would never do such a thing."

"Yeah, well, tell that to your old friend Charlie and see how far it gets you."

The red lights were flashing now. The sheriff stopped a little past Charlie's driveway and waited until they turned, in case they were really trying to steal Charlie's stupid old truck, Grady figured.

Lila drove slowly down the driveway. "Well, at least we got home safe."

As they neared the house, Grady saw Charlie pull back the curtains to watch them. "Yeah," Grady said. "Nothing like home, sweet trusting home."

CHAPTER
7

Lila dropped Grady off at the cottage so he could make the sandwiches while she returned the truck and keys. By the time she got back, he had already polished one off, along with three good-sized fingers of peanut butter on the side. He washed another sandwich down with a glass of milk, then made up his cot in the closet and went to bed. Sleeping in a closet wasn't as bad as it sounded. He could even read by the light of the ceiling bulb if he wanted to. Grady liked the privacy but was glad there was a curtain instead of a real door. At least he wouldn't die in his sleep from lack of air.

And he liked having a spot to call his own, even if it was a room barely big enough to hold his bed. In their first commune he slept in the boys' bunkhouse, and the places after that he always shared a small room with Lila. This was definitely a step up. Charlie Fernwald's farm was turning out to be a six or seven.

Grady must have been tired, because the next thing he knew, he woke in the morning to the smell of something baking. He stuck his head through the curtain door. "Is it pancakes?"

Lila looked up with a spot of flour on her nose. "It's zucchini carrot bread for Charlie."

Grady swung his knees out the door and went over to the table. The linoleum floor was cold on his bare feet. He pulled out the chair near the oven to warm up. Lila shoved the loaf of day-old store bread across the table. "Make yourself some toast. There's jam and peanut butter, if you want it."

"Oh, good, something different," Grady said. "I sure was getting sick of those peanut butter sandwiches."

"Don't give me none of your lip, Grady. I want you to take this up to Charlie soon as you've ate and got dressed."

"Aw, Mom. He's not going to eat any of your veggie stuff."

"Yes, he is, because this bread is as sweet as honey and nobody's going to tell him about those veggies

I hid inside, hear? Hurry up so he gets it while it's still hot."

After Grady had his peanut butter toast sandwich and slid back into his clothes, he headed up to the big house with Lila's bread. She had wrapped it in a few layers of paper towels, but it warmed his fingers as he trudged through the cold.

Charlie was out in the yard, working on one of his antennas. He had lowered the part with the spokes so they were only about chest high and was fastening some big white gourds to the end of each one with wire. Charlie looked over his shoulder when he heard Grady come up behind him. "You need something?"

"No. My mom sent this up for you."

"What's that?"

"Bread. Homemade. It's still hot."

Charlie went back to fastening the gourds to the antenna. "I told your mother she didn't need to cook for me. Take it back and tell her thanks, but no thanks."

"I'm not telling her that. She's going to keep on cooking for you, so you might as well eat it."

Charlie took the bread from Grady, lifted a corner of the paper towel, and sniffed. "What's in it?"

"Nothing that's going to jump out and bite you. It's baking stuff. Butter and sugar and flour, I guess."

Charlie raised his bushy eyebrows. "You sure? I thought your mother was one of those health food nuts."

Grady reached for the bread. Nobody was going to call his mother a nut. "Forget it. I'll eat it. The only food she bought for us was stale bread and lousy peanut butter. The rest was all for you."

"I told you I didn't want her to do that. The money was for your food, not mine."

"Well, she went ahead and done it and she's going to kill me if I bring it home, so I'm going to start eating it right now if you aren't."

Charlie kept a grip on the bread. "Now, don't be so hasty. I could use a break about now. How about we both go in and have a piece of this? Then maybe you could do me a favor by giving me some help with my gourds."

"The way you talk, you're doing me a favor by eating Mom's bread and I return the favor by working for you. Doesn't seem like an even trade to me."

Charlie shrugged and handed back the bread. "I thought you'd like to learn something new. It's all the same to me one way or the other."

Grady took the bread and stormed off toward the barn. He figured he could hunker down out of sight and enjoy his feast. Then he thought of something and ran back to Charlie. "Don't tell my mom I ate this, okay? If she asks, tell her you ate it and you liked it."

Charlie shook his head. "No, I can't do that. I won't tell a lie for anybody. Never did. Never will."

"It's no big deal," Grady said. "It's only a loaf of bread."

"It was a big deal to your mother or she wouldn't have gone to all the trouble of baking it."

Why was he trying to talk some sense into this old coot? Charlie was never going to go along with Lila's plans for him anyway. They should pack up their stuff right now and hitchhike out of town.

Charlie put down the gourd and started walking toward the house. He stopped on the porch steps and turned around. "Are you going to bring that bread or not?"

Now Grady was supposed to be a mind reader? "Yeah, I'm coming."

By the time Grady got to the house, Charlie was putting out two plates. He went to the refrigerator. "You need butter on this bread?"

"Not really. It's sort of like cake."

Charlie's head was in the refrigerator. "You should have told me that in the first place. I never met a cake I didn't like." He opened a carton of milk and smelled it, then held it out. "You think this has gone bad?"

Grady could tell from across the room that it had. The whole refrigerator smelled like it had gone bad. He nodded.

Charlie poured it down the sink. "All I have is coffee. Black. You want that?"

"I don't care." Grady wasn't wild about coffee and Lila had a fit when he drank it, but at least it might warm him up.

"Have a seat, then." Charlie poured two mugs of coffee that looked like used motor oil, then cut the bread, sliding a plate with one piece across the table.

Grady took a sip of coffee. It made him shiver. It was bitter as sucking on a piece of raw rhubarb.

Charlie sat across from him and studied his slice of bread. Grady was hoping he wouldn't notice the little green and orange specks from the zucchini and carrots. He didn't. He broke off a piece and ate it. "Good. It is more like cake than bread. Nice and moist." He polished it off and took more.

They ate in silence. Grady had to take a bite of the

sweet bread after each sip of Charlie's mud coffee, but it did heat up his insides some.

"So . . . are you willing to help me out around here or not?"

"It's my mom you hired. I wasn't in the deal," Grady said.

"No, you weren't. But maybe we can work out our own deal."

Grady bent his head down so his hair fell over his eyes. That way he could watch Charlie without him knowing it. Whenever anybody started talking about making a deal, Grady put his radar into high gear. Lila had been cheated too many times, so it was his job to protect them.

"Every now and then there's a chore around here I could use some help with," Charlie said. "I'd pay by the job, not by the hour. That way you wouldn't be tempted to work slow to make more money."

"You got no right to call me lazy," Grady said. "I'm a hard worker."

Charlie nodded. "Fair enough. We'll figure out the pay for each job, one at a time. You interested?"

"Maybe." Grady shrugged. "Depends on the job . . . and the pay."

Charlie had been watching something out of the

big picture window. All of a sudden he jumped up and grabbed a pair of binoculars, twirling the little knob until he brought something into focus. "Dang! They're back already. I had a feeling they might be early!"

Grady looked out in the driveway but didn't see anything.

Charlie gulped the last of his coffee and grabbed his jacket. "Come on! I'll introduce you."

Grady followed him out on the porch. "Hey, Marie!" Charlie shouted. "Welcome home!"

He was running out to the antennas, looking up, but there was nothing in sight. All of a sudden Grady figured it out. There had been a man at their first commune—Spaceman, they called him—who was always seeing UFOs. He claimed he could bring aliens in for a landing by flapping bedsheets at them. Grady was only a little kid then, and Spaceman had him convinced that a flying saucer with little green men was going to land right in the middle of that commune. Grady practically wore his eyes bloodshot staring at the sky, but never saw a single thing.

Spaceman told Grady he couldn't see the UFOs because he didn't believe in them hard enough. He said if Grady stood out under the stars all night balanced on one leg, those aliens would see he was sincere and they'd make themselves visible to him. Grady tried. Lord, how he tried. But he couldn't keep his balance for more than a few minutes at a time. After about an hour, Spaceman showed up with a bunch of other guys and shone a flashlight on Grady on one leg with his arms pinwheeling to keep balanced. Everybody had laughed. What a rotten trick to play on a little kid.

Grady never did find out if Spaceman really believed in aliens or if he was just playing a joke, because after Lila heard about what had happened she packed up and they left the next morning. "Ain't nobody going to treat my boy like that," she had said.

That's when Grady learned that you had to watch out for people. "Don't trust nobody right off until you get to know 'em," Lila had told him. "And even then, you got to keep an eye on 'em. There's good people in this world and there's bad people, but ain't no tellin' which is which by their looks." Grady had remembered that advice and followed it. Unfortunately, Lila's trusting nature often made her forget her own wise words.

Grady watched old Charlie Fernwald dancing

around the yard under the poles, waving his arms and calling out to his imaginary friends in the sky. So that's what the weird antennas were for. Charlie was trying to lure in aliens with his contraptions. No wonder Roger wanted somebody to baby-sit his father. Charlie Fernwald was crazy as a stinkbug on a hot sidewalk.

CHAPTER
8

Grady tried to slip past Charlie and go back to the cottage, but he wasn't fast enough. "Hey, don't run off when I have a job for you, boy. Give me a hand here."

A job? Grady didn't want to get roped into Charlie's fantasy world. On the other hand, if there was some money involved, he'd be a fool to pass it up. What could it hurt, anyway? He could humor the old guy and end up with some spare change in his pocket.

Charlie must have read his mind. "Twenty-five cents for each gourd you fasten to the rack. Deal?"

Grady did some fast mental math. There were three poles with eight spokes on each one. Charlie had put six gourds on the first pole. So that left eight times two—sixteen, plus two—eighteen, divided by four— four dollars and fifty cents.

"You just going to stand there, or do we have a deal?"

"Deal."

It wasn't hard work. Each gourd had a thick plastic-covered wire threaded through two holes in the top. Charlie showed Grady how to wind each end of the wire along the spoke. "Leave a little play in it so the gourd can swing some. They like that."

"Oh, I bet they do," Grady said. "Must be like a little carnival ride for 'em." Figured he might as well play along. Charlie gave him a funny look but didn't say anything. Grady had three gourds fastened up in no time. One more and he'd have a dollar. "What are those funny-shaped holes in the front for?" Grady asked.

"Each gourd has an entrance hole for them to get inside," Charlie said. "It's shaped like a crescent to keep their enemies from getting in."

"What about the Batman-shaped holes?" Grady was picturing little green aliens in tights and capes.

"Same thing," Charlie said. "They're new. I'm trying them out to see which ones work best. Then I'll send in a report at the end of the season."

Grady grinned. "To galaxy headquarters?"

"What's that you say?"

Grady didn't want to get Charlie upset before he

was paid. "Nothing. I'm counting my quarters." Man! This guy thought he had space wars going on in his own backyard. "So what does the enemy look like?" Grady asked, egging Charlie on.

"I've got pictures in the house," Charlie said. "I'll show you later."

Pictures, huh? This was going to be fun. In spite of the fact that he knew it was crazy, Grady felt himself being drawn back into the old excitement of seeing little green men from outer space. After all, it was a big universe. Nobody had ever proved that they *didn't* exist. And Grady was too old and too smart to get tricked by Charlie if he was playing a joke.

Charlie picked up his binoculars again. "They show up, then take right off. Trying to make me think they're not going to stay here. They'll be back, though. They always come back. You ever seen them?"

Should he admit to his UFO experience? Sure, why not? It would be interesting to see what Charlie would say. "Almost. I mean I knew someone who could see them, but I didn't."

"What in tarnation are you talking about, boy? Either you've seen martins or you haven't."

Martins? That was funny. Charlie couldn't even pronounce *martians* right. Old Charlie Fernwald wasn't as smart as he pretended to be. That made Grady feel better—less vulnerable. He went over to the pile of gourds and grabbed a couple more. An easy fifty cents.

Charlie had finished loading the second pole and came over to help Grady with the last one. "Poor things have had a long trip. They spend their winters in Brazil. And they come back to the same house every year. Sure is a big day when they come back. There's not a sight in the world prettier than a flock of purple martins."

"Purple? I thought they were green."

"Being smart now, are you?" Charlie shook his head. "After my wife died, I thought my life was over, then Roger got me my first gourd rack. Most people around here have a hard time attracting martins. Not me. Four days after I put up the rack, in they came. I've been a purple martin landlord ever since."

All of a sudden a small dark shape tumbled out of the sky and skimmed so close to Grady's face, he could feel the breeze on his cheek.

"It's Marie!" Charlie yelled. "She's usually one of the first ones back. She's after you because you're holding her gourd. Better hurry. We still need to put the pine needles in."

The thing swooped at Grady again, and this time he swatted at it. Charlie caught his wrist. "What's the matter with you? I won't have you hurting my birds."

Birds? Grady looked up. There were five of them circling overhead, making a bright chattering sound. While Grady was standing there with his mouth open, Charlie fastened on the last of the gourds. Then he started unscrewing caps on the side of each gourd and stuffing pine needles inside. "Come on," he said, grabbing a handful of needles out of a bushel basket. "They're getting impatient. Put two or three inches of needles in each gourd."

"What for?" Grady asked.

"Nests," Charlie said. "We're making nests for them."

"Don't birds usually build their own nests?"

Charlie screwed the last cap back on and started cranking the gourds up the pole with a winch. "These aren't usual birds. Besides, they're tired. They've just flown in from Brazil, remember? I like to give them a soft bed to sleep on."

The birds were landing on the rack before it reached the top of the pole. Charlie raised up the last rack. "Here it comes, Marie. Gourd number twenty-one. Home, sweet home." Even before the gourds stopped moving, the bird Charlie called Marie folded her wings close to her body and dove into the entrance hole marked twenty-one.

Charlie's face was red, either from excitement or all the rushing around. "Isn't that a sight? Every year they find their way back to my farm."

There were more birds overhead now. "How do you know they're the same birds as last year? They all look alike to me."

"I can't tell most of them apart, but I know Marie. First off, she always claims the same gourd. And if you look closely, you'll see she's the only one with a band on her leg."

"Did you put that on her?"

"No, you have to be a licensed bander to do that. It was probably done at her first colony where she hatched and fledged. Probably someplace thirty to fifty miles from here."

"Then why did she come here? I thought you said they always go back to the same house."

"I've read that only about one out of ten martins return to their original colony the second year. I'm not sure why that is, but it's a good thing, because that's how new colonies get started. The second year martins are looking for a place to live, and from then on they stay loyal to their new colony. Anyway, Marie has always been my favorite. She's the best acrobat. Her antics will make you laugh right out loud."

Grady wasn't sure if he was disappointed or relieved that Charlie's visitors were only birds. Not that he had really believed in aliens, but after all the buildup, this was pretty tame. Maybe when you got to be an old geezer, you could get all worked up about bird watching, but it sure wasn't Grady's idea of a good time. Now he was wondering if Charlie would really pay up. He stood around for a few minutes, hoping Charlie would remember the money, but the old man was too involved with his birds to think about anything else. Grady stepped closer. "I guess I'm all through here now. I'd better go back and see if Mom needs anything."

Charlie was barely listening to him, keeping his eyes glued on those darn birds. "All right." He gave a halfhearted wave—a gesture of dismissal. Grady waited to see that hand reach for his wallet. Nothing.

Grady cleared his throat. "I mean unless you have another *job* for me to do."

That remark brought Charlie out of his bird trance. "Oh, right, I owe you some money here. How many gourds did you do?"

"Six, I think. Maybe seven." Grady wished he had

been faster. All that time he'd wasted staring, he could have been earning more quarters. Next time he'd be smarter.

Charlie pulled out two dollar bills.

"I don't have change," Grady said.

Charlie smiled. "So you'll owe me a quarter. Thanks for the help."

Before Grady could answer, Charlie was talking to his birds again.

Well, he wasn't another UFO nut, but believing these birds flew back and forth to Brazil every year was as crazy as thinking aliens were landing in the yard. The old guy was probably harmless, though, and for the first time in his life, Grady had a little spending money of his own.

CHAPTER
9

Lila was pleased pink that Charlie had liked her bread. "Didn't I tell you, Grady? There's no way he could resist my bread fresh from the oven like that. Why, that aroma grabs your taste buds in a stranglehold."

"Kinda hard to swallow that way, isn't it?" Grady asked.

Lila gave him a gentle punch on the arm. "Never mind, smart mouth. You know I'm a good cook. And tonight I'm going to make Charlie Fernwald the best dinner he ever ate."

"Don't push your luck, Mom. Maybe he liked the bread, but that doesn't mean he's going to let you cook him dinner."

Lila stood at the open refrigerator door, studying

its contents. "Leave me be, Grady. I'm figuring out a menu."

"Well, whatever you make, you better freeze it in a little cardboard box he can heat up in his microwave, or he's not going to eat it. That man is real set in his ways."

A sudden knock on the door made them both jump. Lila peeked out the window. "It's him," she whispered. "Don't you say nothing to upset him."

Grady sighed. "He probably wants me to help with his birds again."

Lila smoothed back her hair and opened the door. "Well, isn't this a nice surprise. You just come right on in here, Mr. Fernwald, and make yourself to home." She gestured toward the only comfortable chair in the room.

Charlie stood in the doorway. He was so tall, the house seemed built for elves. Funny, he wasn't stooped over like most of the old geezers Grady had seen. "No need for me to come in. I wondered if you could do me a favor."

Grady shot him a sideways glance. Here it comes, Grady thought. He's got something else for me to do, but if he calls it a favor, there won't be any pay. Grady moved to the far corner of the room—an empty gesture because it was only three steps away.

"I'd surely be pleased to do you a favor," Lila said, her face all bright and smiley. "You tell me what it is, and it's as good as done."

"Well, I was wondering . . ." Charlie had taken off his John Deere cap and was working his fingers around the brim. "My son and his wife have invited themselves over tomorrow. They're coming around one o'clock."

"I suspect they want to see how good a cook I am. I think we should give them a fine Sunday dinner, don't you?"

Charlie smiled and nodded. He seemed relieved not to have to say it himself. "Just because it's Sunday dinner doesn't mean you have to go all out, though. Anything will be fine. And this doesn't mean I want you to start cooking for me. It's a onetime favor."

Lila raised her eyebrows and sent a smug look across the room to Grady. "Now, that's no favor at all. It's what I was hired for in the first place."

"Oh, and one more thing," Charlie said. "Could you make sure you cook a vegetable? Roger's wife, Ethel, is still fussing about me staying here alone. If she sees me eating vegetables, that should win her over. Try to make it something that tastes halfway decent, though. Nothing green."

"Well, vegetables just happen to be my specialty. I can make an acorn squash taste better than a hot fudge sundae."

Grady tried not to smile. He knew that statement was a big exaggeration.

Charlie seemed dubious, too. "Pretty sure of yourself, aren't you?"

"I don't mean to sound prideful, Mr. Fernwald. I'm only speaking the honest truth."

"I guess I'll be the judge of that." Charlie reached in his pocket and handed Lila some money. "I suppose you'll need to get extra food in. Will this cover it?"

"It surely will, because I pride myself on being good at spotting a bargain. Not that I ever skimp on quality, but I can make a dollar go farther than anybody you ever met."

Grady's sigh made Charlie notice him for the first time. "Have you been watching my birds, Grady? You can see them from your front window, can't you?"

"You didn't say I had to watch them."

"Tarnation, you don't *have* to watch them. I thought you'd *like* to. They're pretty interesting. Better than watching TV."

"We don't *have* a TV," Grady said. He was still annoyed about that.

Charlie put his cap back on his head. "Then I guess you're lucky to have the martins to keep you entertained." Charlie closed the door before Grady could think of a comeback. He wasn't about to watch any stupid birds. Not unless he got paid good money to do it.

When Lila went off to buy the food, Grady stayed in the cottage. He made up his cot in the closet, smoothing out the bedspread. Then he propped up his pillows and stretched out. A long horizontal board against the back wall made a narrow shelf just about eye level when he was sitting up. Grady hung over the edge of the bed and pulled out his backpack. He could put his stuff on that shelf, make things more homelike. He lined up his toothbrush, a small plastic comb, his book, and the red Corvette Matchbox car his dad had given him the last Christmas he was alive.

Grady's dad was always on the lookout for an old Corvette he could fix up, but he never had found one he could afford, except for one that was smashed beyond repair. Grady had known there was something special in that tiny package on that last Christmas morning. He could tell by the way his father watched him open it. "Someday," his dad said, "I'll find us a real Corvette, Grady. And you and me will fix it up so it runs good as new. Then we'll paint it candy apple red, just like this one."

Now, as he ran that little car across the shelf, Grady's eyes stung with the tears he never showed to anybody. He could picture his father at the wheel, laughing. What a time they would have had in that car. How different their lives would have been if it hadn't been for the accident. Grady shook his head and pushed the memories aside. Feeling sorry for himself only made things worse. He parallel parked the Corvette between the comb and the toothbrush, then leaned back on his pillows and looked at his tiny room. It wasn't bad, now that he had his stuff out where he could see it. It felt more like home than anywhere he'd been in a long time. This place could be a seven and a half or an eight.

The next day, Grady helped Lila lug the groceries up to the kitchen in the big house. "I'm going to need about forty-five minutes to myself, Grady. Your job is to keep that man out of his kitchen while I'm trying to cook."

"How am I supposed to do that?"

"I don't know. Ask him about those birds of his. That'll keep him going for a while. I don't want him coming in here snooping around."

Grady went into the living room. Charlie was sitting at the table with a pen in his hand and a notebook in front of him, looking out the window at his birds. He glanced up when Grady came into the room. "Have a seat. They're all flying around the gourds now. Putting on a good show. Look how they swoop around on those graceful wings of theirs."

Grady plopped into the chair opposite Charlie. There were a couple dozen birds now from what Grady could see. "More of 'em came, huh?" Good. Question number one. That wasn't hard. Only about forty-four more bird questions ought to fill the time until dinner.

Charlie took the bait for question number one.

"This is only half of what we'll get if it's a good year. We've got housing up for forty-eight."

Grady noticed Charlie was talking in terms of "we," as if the birds were partly his. "Oh, so you get two birds to each house?"

"Well, sure. You need a pair. A male and a female."

Rats! That was a stupid question and it didn't take up much time. Grady's mind was racing to find a third question but he didn't need to. Charlie was off and running. He pushed the notebook across the table. "This gives all the numbers from last year and the dates they arrived. They're right on schedule. I've been watching their progress on the Internet, too. The first wave is about ready to cross over Lake Erie to Canada."

"They show that on the Internet?"

"Yep. The first reports always come from Florida— Naples and Marco Island in late December or early January. Then by late January they're showing up in Texas—Corpus Christi and San Antonio. Seems like it's easier to get martins down South. They say you hang up an old boot in Texas and the martins will move right in. Up here there aren't nearly as many martins, so it's more of a challenge. Some people try for years and never get them. Come on, I'll show you the scout report map."

Grady followed Charlie into a small room with a computer on a desk. Funny, he didn't think of an old guy like Charlie having a computer. "You got any games on this?" he asked.

"Don't have time for games," Charlie said. "I use it for e-mail and the purple martin forum. And researching anything else I need to know."

Grady looked around the room. All four walls were filled with bookshelves. He'd never seen so many books in somebody's house before. "Wow! This is like a library."

Charlie sat down and turned on the computer. "I guess it is. We never had much of a library in town, so I started buying my own books years ago. Picked up a lot of these at secondhand book stores when I used to travel some."

"Where is the library in town?" Grady asked.

"There isn't one now. They combined with the big one over in Addieville. That's almost fifteen miles away. Seems a shame folks have to go so far to get a book."

Grady's heart fell. He was hoping he'd be able to

walk to a library. He wouldn't have minded walking to town from here to get a book. But fifteen miles, that was another thing altogether.

There hadn't been a library in the nearest town to Sunward Path, and the school at the commune was a joke. They were supposed to have class every day, but Rayden was the official teacher and he was more interested in himself than the kids, only holding one or two classes a week and then mostly rambling on with his "philosophizing," as Lila called it. Or sometimes he'd have the kids make stuff for the commune to sell. The last project was candle making. Since handling melted wax was too dangerous for the younger kids, Grady did most of the work. That took up three whole "school" days, and Rayden kept all the profits from selling the candles.

Charlie got up and pulled a book off the shelf. "Here's a good bird guide. It has a whole section on swallows. That's what purple martins are, you know. We have them all here—barn swallows, cliff swallows, and tree swallows." Charlie was flipping through the pages, pointing to different birds. They all looked the same to Grady. You've seen one bird, you've seen 'em all.

"These are the ones you have to watch out for," Charlie was saying, "the tree swallows. If you let a pair nest in your martin housing, they'll chase off all your martins. That's what that gourd on the short pole is for. I have a pair of tree swallows nesting in that now. They're so territorial, they'll chase off all the other tree swallows, so now it's clear sailing for the martins."

Grady looked out at the lower gourd. Sure enough, there was a dark blue and white head sticking out of the entrance hole. "How did you make the tree swallows go into the right house?" This was a real question—not that he was interested in birds. Just curious.

Charlie was back at the computer. "It's all on the Internet. The PMCA—Purple Martin Conservation Association—has a Web site with a message board. You got a question, somebody will have the answer. Look, here's the Scout Arrival study or, as some of us purple martin landlords call it, the 'Purple Wave.' Pull up that other chair."

There was a map of the United States on the screen that looked like somebody had spilled grape syrup on it. A wavy line spread north from the Gulf of Mexico. "Here's where we are," Charlie said, pointing at the screen near the top edge of the grape spill. "The best time is when the wave is almost up to where you live. It's like waiting for Christmas."

Grady wasn't sure what to think. If it was only Charlie going on about his birds, Grady could dismiss him as being a nut. But there must be lots of people wild about purple martins if they had a whole Web site and a real organization. Grady leaned in to get a better look. "Where are we, anyway?"

"I showed you. The town is called Bedelia."

"Yeah, I know that, but what state are we in?"

Charlie glanced over his shoulder. "I'd say you're in a state of confusion. This is Pennsylvania. Don't they teach geography in the schools anymore?"

"Well, we've moved around a lot, so I don't always get a whole year in one school. And we didn't learn nothing in the commune school."

"Commune!" Charlie spun his chair all the way around to face him. "Tarnation! They still have hippies? I thought they went out in the sixties."

Grady could feel his face getting hot. "We're not hippies. I told you, we move a lot, is all. And I'm not dumb. Once I read about something, I don't forget it."

"Well, then we'd better get you some reading material. Here, start with this atlas of the United States. And here's a bird book. What else are you interested in?"

Grady looked around at the shelves. There were lots of things that interested him—a book about wolves, another about airplanes, and the Chilton's auto mechanic's manual like the one his father had owned. He pulled that one off the shelf.

"You interested in fixing cars, are you?"

"Maybe," Grady said.

"You could start on an old tractor. That's what I did when I was your age. I have one back of the barn you could work on with me. I want to get it running good enough to sell."

"You're a mechanic?" Grady asked, trying to picture Charlie under a car.

"Every farmer's a mechanic. You have to be. When your tractor goes down in the middle of planting, you can't wait for somebody to come fix it." Charlie pulled another book from the shelf and rubbed the dust off the spine. "Here's some other books you might like. This section by the window has some books I got for my grandson when he was a kid. Fiction, mostly. That's the only part that's organized. You can borrow anything you want, long as you take care of it and bring it back when you're finished. Understand?"

Grady couldn't imagine anybody owning so many books. This was like having his own library. If he ever had a house someday, he was going to line the walls with books exactly like this.

"Guess I'll go in and see how your mother is doing with the meal," Charlie said.

Grady was so intent on looking at the books, Charlie was out of the room before he realized what was happening. He came to his senses in time to head Charlie off right before the kitchen. "I'll go see if Mom needs help. That's supposed to be my job. I'm her assistant."

"Well, I was only going to take a peek. Something smells pretty good."

Grady blocked the kitchen door. "Yeah, well, Mom doesn't like to have people watching her when she cooks."

"Oh, an artiste, is she?"

"Something like that."

"All right. I don't want to cramp her style." Charlie went back to the table with his bird notebook. "Remind her that Roger and Ethel will be here at one. They're always prompt. Sometimes early. I think Ethel wants to catch me doing something senile so she can put me in a home."

Charlie grinned, so Grady realized he was joking. Grady grinned back at him. "Okay, I'll tell her."

When Grady got into the kitchen, he could see why Lila didn't want Charlie in there. She was sneaking vegetables into everything—green vegetables.

"Aw, Mom, what are you doin' that for? Can't you cook something normal?"

"Grady, I may only have one chance to get some vitamins into that man, and I'm going to squeeze in as many as possible."

"But brussels sprouts? He's gonna taste them for sure. You want him to throw up in front of his son? That'll get you fired."

"Don't you worry your head about that. I can hide anything in a nice seasoned sauce." Lila shoved the brussels sprouts and some spinach into the blender and spun them into a green mush. Then she poured the stuff into a pot.

"Oh, yeah. He's goin' to love that. Smells like something that came out the back of a lawn mower."

"You get out of here and let me work. And keep that man busy, hear?"

"Yeah, I hear."

Twenty-four hours ago, Grady wouldn't have cared if Lila got fired. They could move on to another place, maybe better, maybe worse. But now he wasn't sure he wanted to go. If he could have all those books to read . . . if he could work on repairing a tractor . . . well, there was no sense getting worked up over it. He had learned long ago that it didn't pay to get attached to things or people, because he couldn't count on anything to stay the way it was for long. As Lila always said, "Enjoy what you have when you have it. Not one single thing in this world lasts forever."